JUNGKOOK'S STORY OF 35 DAYS

BARIRA AND NAMRA

this book is fiction .. so that each bts army should not be upset after reading this book . I , barira khan always wants to write a book with my cousin namra ... and finally this time it hapened ! my cousin is also intrested in writing a small novel with me or you can even say i force her to ..... hehehe ....

so without wasting pages and time lets proceed !

Contents

Preface

so , i am barira khan author of this book . i am 12 years old and i always have a dream to be famous as j.k. rowling and elon musk .....out of tis' i would like to telll everone something ...... that my cousin is also writing this masterpiece with me .. quite intresting ....

namra shahzad is her name and her role is as a co- author here she is also 12 years old and my bestest friend ... she also like kpop and fashion designing is her dream .. but as time passes she is also intresting in writing a book with me !

its namra's first time but mine second .... so barira khan .. i'm tyoing and she is giving me ideas side-by-side .

Prologue

ceo jungkook ! and park eun byeol the girl which jungkook injured with a permanent scar !

park eun byeol claims that the ceo kookie is her boyfriend . she was going through a mental disorder in which she feels weired with mens .... but not with jk because kookie saved her from her cheater boyfriend .

introduction of kookie

kosmetik company ! ceo jungkook claims it ! .... what is this why my company name is so cheap .. it has to be kookies makeover ! change it over night said ceo jungkook to assistant park eun byeol . ms park said " o....ok.. s.s. sir " . jungkook noded his head to proof that he heard her .

    ms park change the name over night when jungkook was working on a serum that can hide the scar ....

ms park's bf

ms park was also a delivery girl at momo's restaurant. she had an order of chickn nuggets and french fries .... the address is of her own house so she got scared . she go there with the order and saw that her boyfriend and some girls are on her bed .... so she cried and run out of the house .. it was korean bridge where she and her boyfriend met .... she ran away and hit by the car of ceo jungkook . that boyfried was also with jungkook so he told his guards to arrest him . ms park was faint and homeless at the time . because she live with her boyfried after her parents death ...... she has no one in this life except from ceo jungkook 's company ... jungkook take her to the hospital and her forehead was bleeding insanely .

after she awake she saw jungkook giving a hard punch to her boyfriend .... ms park said '' mr jungkook ! please stop it ! ...... he is my boyfriend not your punching bag ! jungkook aid he cheated you , so how could i not . she said i dont have any other home to live in . jungkook think a while and take ms park to his home ....

his home is full of luxury items and also have a huge garden that is full of rosses . she entered her room and straight to the bed .... jungkook said '' dont find difficulty in living in my room , its quite large so dont just be on bed , just go inside the garden and pluck some flowers for you . smirk* by ms park

foundation or serum treatment

the foundation is more powerful then a serum said chairmen smith , but jungkook like serum because after foundation the face looks un moisturized ..... he then take the permission of chaimen to change the topic !

topic serum ... now jungkook has to work on that ! with ms park and mrs kim ji hoo . mrs kim ji hoo is one of the best dermatoligist in the country of korea . mrs kim , mr jeon and ms park are on the same project . soon they all have a grand idea to set up a show in which various people will show their talent of makeover . mrs kim is the host and mr jeon and ms park were the judge ! mr jungkook knows all the science behind makeup chemicals and ms park is best in reseach of chemicals . now the show was set up in china the state near the great wall .

show and expose

the first step of the show is show and expose . in which participents has to show the natural beauty of theirselves , mr jeon jungkook force ms park to participate in the show so that she can be more confident in herself . after removing the make up ms park got exposed live ! she has a big scar on her cheek .

mr jungkook got worried and tries to hide her .... ms park got embarresed and cried because of jungkook .

at night she tried to ran away from mr jungkook's house but cant because of guards all around this room .... then she saw the news and it was ended up their , their rumors were created that how could mr jungkook more that 50% shareholder of his company can do so .... every one saw his as a cold ceo ... but he is so proctective .

everyone wants to protect ms park but can't because of mrs kim . she likes jungkook so much from childhood but whenever she moves a step foreword jungkook moves ten steps back .

mrs kim has a news channel in which she creates thousands of romurs against two person dating .

now her evel eyes are on ms park ....

jungkook is in his bathroom crying because he finally found the girl he is looking for ... after 15 years .

breaking news !

breaking news ! jungkook and ms park are dating ! mrs park eun byeol wants to be mrs jeon eun byeol .

jungkook ! said ms park . jungkook was so upset after mrs kim ji hoo uploads a live video of their show exposing ms park

then mrs kim invites mr jungkook on her birthday and jungkook has not attend because she has not invite ms park

after some days mr jungkook arrange a lunch with mrs park ji hoo and then in that lunch ms park was also their , mrs kim ji hoo came with her husband mr shin sam kuro , he is japanese and knows well about climatic conditions over the world . he is also a lifestyle influencer and one of the most respected person at airport as his dad was a pilot but now mr shin sam kuro is orphan .

at lunch

mr jungkook introduced his wife with mr and mrs kim , and it as ms park eun byeol !

park eun byeol and mr jungkook marry that morning and thei have not even changed their dresses .mrs kim was shocked ! that how could mms park does it .... she then cried intront of everyon , shin sam kuro then slap her because mr jungkook told him everything . then shin sam kuro claimed that her wife does not love him . she loves mr jungkook . the mrs kim said sorry to mrs park , mr jungkook and mr shin sam kuro then shin sam kuro said just like i am orphan mrs park is also orphan , you don't know how much it pains when it was parents day and you don't have both . then mrs kim said sorry to shin s. kuro and also to mrs park infront of whole media .

the real case

how does mrs park hert ? said mrs kim to everyone at lunch . then jungkook told them that during his school times he got bully and mrs park to ... so to save her i use to frighten those bully but i by mistake fell down an hert her cheek .... from that day she never attend the school and i have not even say sorry to her .

mrs kim said why did mrs park do so ? she said because of my grandmothers death i was transfered from orea to england .

mrs kim said ..... so its the time ! jungkook ! ..... jungkook said " for what " . mrs kim said " to say sorry to mrs park and make the serun for her to hide the scar ". mr jungkook was impresed by her words and say sorry to mrs park . then all of them work on their project .

the serum is ....

the serum is ready ! said mr jungkook ... he tried it on his wife mrs park and it was hide sucessfully ... mrs park and mrs kim were happy and by the time passes the scar became invisible an then all of a sudden her skim become so soft , moisturized and super hydrating . she thanked mr jungkook and mrs kim for it and sai " without you both it can't be happened "

it was the best ending ever !!!!!!

Ending

always the happiest of all
    for my nam nam ; you are my serum and i am your chemical
    nam nam love you